A party for Brown Mouse

Story by Jenny Giles   Illustrations by Pat DeWitt-Grush

"It is my birthday today,"
said Brown Mouse
to White Mouse.
"You can come to my party."

"Oh, thank you," said White Mouse.
"I will come to your party."

"Here comes the cat!"
said Brown Mouse.
"He will eat you!
Run in here!"

Brown Mouse said to Gray Mouse,
"You can come
to my party, too."

"Oh, thank you," said Gray Mouse.
"I will come to your party."

"Here comes the cat!"

said Brown Mouse.

"He will eat you! Run in here!"

"Here is the party,"
said Brown Mouse.

"I like bread and cheese!"
said White Mouse.

"I like cake," said Gray Mouse.
"Where is your birthday cake?"

"Here is my birthday cake!"
said Brown Mouse.
"Look! It is a cat cake."

Happy birthday to you,

Happy birthday to you,

Happy birthday to Brown Mouse,

Happy birthday to you.

"Come on," said Brown Mouse.

"We will eat the **cat**!"